My Perfect Neighborhood

by Leah Komaiko

illustrated by Barbara Westman

Harper & Row, Publishers

Library of Congress Cataloging-in-Publication Data
Komaiko, Leah.
   My perfect neighborhood / by Leah Komaiko ; illustrated by Barbara
Westman.
       p.   cm.
   Summary: A little girl takes a walk in her urban neighborhood and
delights in its quirky personality.
   ISBN 0-06-023287-0 : $. — ISBN 0-06-023288-9 (lib. bdg.) :
$
   {1. Neighborhood—Fiction.   2. Stories in rhyme.}   I. Westman,
Barbara, ill.   II. Title.
PZ8.3.K835My 1990   89-37871
{E}—dc20   CIP
                                                                    AC

Typography by Christine Kettner
1   2   3   4   5   6   7   8   9   10
First Edition

For Barbara Karlin and
Rockin' Robin Weisman
L.K.

For Arthur
B.W.

I went out for a walk today.
My neighborhood she looked okay.

The dogs waved when the cats marched by.

The builders built a brick-cream pie

And clothes hung in the trees to dry.
My neighborhood's the place to try.

I went out for a walk today.
My neighborhood she looked okay.
The grown-ups lined up for recess.

The poodles found a wedding dress

And birds played bongos, more or less.
This neighborhood's the best address.

I went out for my walk today.
My neighborhood she looked okay.

A horse was out on roller skates.

My grandmother was lifting weights
And dishwashers were juggling plates.
I told you, this place really rates.

I went out for my walk today
And saw the sights that came my way:
The dentist shaving someone's head,

The baker baking sweet-tooth bread,
And bed salesmen, asleep in bed.
This place is special, like I said.

I went out for my walk today
And saw...*myself*....I looked okay.

My legs were each a half arm high.
My elbow almost touched my thigh
And half my nose was in my eye.
Oh, what a gorgeous girl am I!

I love my walks, for then I see
That things are just as they should be.